"Michael J. Rubel captures the wonder of the wild and the innocence of childhood imagination. His ability to blend adventure, humor, and heart is remarkable. Benny the Badger teaches important lessons about loyalty, family, and coexistence in the most delightful way."
~*Dr. Jonathan Ellis, Wildlife Conservationist and Author of "Wild Neighbors"*

"Few authors can engage both children and adults the way Rubel does. His storytelling bridges generations children love his characters, and grandparents appreciate the values behind them. Benny the Badger at Bearberry Pass is destined to become a family favorite."
~*Sarah Whitmore, Founder of Family Reading Circle*

"Michael Rubel's stories remind us of a simpler time, filled with curiosity, courage, and kindness. His attention to animal behavior and his gentle humor make every page sparkle. Benny the Badger is not just a book, it's an experience that inspires respect for nature."
~*Emily Ross, Children's Author and Environmental Storyteller*

Benny the Badger **at Bearberry Pass**

Author: Michael J Rubel

1 Via Burrone, Newport Coast, CA 92657

www.booksbyrubel.com

Copyright © 2025 Michael J Rubel
All rights reserved

ISBN:

979-8-89604-345-4 (Paperback)

No part of this publication may be reproduced, distributed, or transmitted in any form or by any means, including photocopying, recording, or other electronic or mechanical methods, without the prior written permission of the author, except in the case of brief quotations embodied in critical reviews and certain other noncommercial uses permitted by copyright law. For permission requests, write to the publisher at the address provided.

OTHER BOOKS BY MICHAEL RUBEL

* *The adventures of Charlie Chipmunk*
* *Big Feet the Story*
* *Charlie's Wild Ride*
* *A Moment in Time (Coming Soon)*

Dedication

This book is dedicated primarily to the animals depicted herein who learn they can live together in harmony. It is also dedicated to my nine grandchildren who will always have these memories of stories told to them over the years.

Table of Contents

Dedication v

The Beginning 1

A Surprise Guest 6

The Garden 10

Lunch with Monica 15

The Coyotes 20

A Mate for Benny 25

Another picnic and a Rescue 29

A Badger Family 33

The Reunion 37

Honey Badger 40

Coyote 42

Acknowledgement 44

About The Author 45

The Beginning

A young badger named Benny lay at the opening of the family burrow and watched the sky in the east turn a dull gray, which was a prelude to another day on Bear Berry Pass, Texas. Soon the sun would rise over the roof of the farmhouse in the distance and warm him as he lay there and waited for his parents to return from their hunting trip. They had never been gone more than two days, and today would be number seven. Surely something had happened to them because they had never failed to bring him food to nourish the young animal. His heart sank at the thought that they would never return and he would be alone in the world.

He had eaten some dried fruit and nuts that were in the burrow, but it was not enough to fill his tummy, which growled at him like another animal inside him. As the sky brightened to a light blue just before sunrise, he slid out of the burrow and walked a short distance to a spring that was located deeper in the forest. He quenched his thirst, but it did not replace something good to eat provided by his mother and father upon their return. Am I alone? he thought, forever? He couldn't stand imagining his parents might have left him, could they?

Benny remembered a large blackberry bush that grew alongside the country road that led to San Antonio to the south. His father had taken him there a few weeks ago, and he thought about the sweet berries that hung low to the ground and could be easily picked by the short, squat badger.

Benny made his way along the edge of the pine forest and through the pasture and soon arrived at the roadway and the berry bushes that lay on the other side. He listened carefully for any cars and then scurried across the road and slid under the bushes to hide.

It was late Fall, and the remaining berries were very ripe. Benny spent the next half hour munching on the wild blackberries and tried not to think about his parents. He was saddened by the loss and hoped one day to see them again, but for now, he was on his own. He prayed that one day his parents would return home and they would be together again as a happy family.

Weeks went by, and his parents never returned. Benny knew that winter would soon come because the wind was colder and blew harder with dark clouds that covered the sky with an occasional rainstorm that soaked him and made him shiver from the cold. For now, he managed to catch some things to eat. It was enough to keep his tummy from grumbling, but not enough to prepare him for the winter that would limit many of the food sources he now ate. Fortunately, badgers also eat plants, and Benny was able to find wild oats and berries that lined the country roads to fill his tummy for a while. He really liked the large blackberry bushes because he could hide under the bush and pick the very ripe berries. He also found nice hiding places under the cover of the bushes, where he could sleep and feel comfortable and safe.

One day, as he lay under the berry bush, he heard singing and looked down the road and saw a young girl as she walked down the pathway that led to the blackberry bushes. The song was pleasurable to Benny's ears. He moved further into the bush to hide, but could still hear her beautiful voice.

    She was carrying a shiny metal bucket under one arm and was smiling and walking along, swinging the bucket and singing. The young girl was from the farmhouse down the road, and he was afraid that she might see him and be frightened. She came closer and stopped about 20 feet from Benny's hiding place. She began picking the berries that were higher on the branches than Benny could reach and started putting them in the bucket. She continued to hum her song as she picked the ripe berries, but occasionally, she would eat one of them and smile at their sweet taste.

    He remembered seeing the girl months ago as she played outside in the yard by the barn with a doll under her arm. Benny was with his father at the time, and he told him to look at the window of the farmhouse facing the garden. Benny was shocked to see a bearded man as he peered out the window and watched his daughter as she played in the yard. His father said that people were not to be trusted since the man had shot his gun at the wild animals in the forest a while ago. Both he and Benny moved back into the cover of the pasture grass and out of sight of the farmer.

    Now, as she moved along the road closer to Benny, he sensed she knew the badger was there. She seemed to look into the berry bushes and smiled, but continued to sing and pick the berries, and didn't seem to mind that Benny was there. Finally, she moved along, and Benny was relieved that she was away from his hiding spot. The afternoon slowly passed, and Benny slept peacefully in the cover of the blackberry bushes. He awoke from a pleasant dream and stretched his arms and legs. He peered outside, and it was late in the evening, and soon it would be dark. He longed for his favorite home burrow and was anxious to find it in the moonlit night. It had been too long since he was there, and it made him smile to remember all the family things he had done with his parents while they lived there.

He left the safety of the bushes and began to hunt for something more suitable than the berries. He searched through the shrubs and was happy to find some mice to catch. Benny was exhausted after spending the entire night searching for food, and continued to feel sorrow over being left by his parents to survive independently. He had been hunting with his father and mother many times, looking for things to eat, so he had an idea what to do. So far, he had been successful enough to feed himself but not enough to get him fat for the winter.

The nights were beginning to get cold, especially s i n c e Bearberry Pass was in the hill country of Central Texas. The wind began to pick up again, and he was anxious to get back to his home. His mother and father had dug a deep burrow alongside a fallen oak tree in the forest, alongside the large pasture. He had been away for three days hunting and sleeping under logs or heavy brush for cover. Last night, he had been frightened when a rattlesnake slithered up to Benny and smelled him with its tongue, and had learned that badgers were not something to deal with, and sensed that this animal would kill them for food. But tonight, the young badger lay there in fright as the snake slithered away. He soon went back to sleep, but was afraid of animals that might harm him. During the early morning, a large hawk swooped down from a tall tree and dove for Benny, who, when he heard the swoosh of wings, ducked under a bush. The hawk was just trying to scare Benny, since both animals ate the same type of food, and the badger was in the hawk's territory.

A Surprise Guest

Benny finally drew close to his home burrow and was relieved to know he was safe and could rest comfortably before he had to hunt again for food. But this time it was a little different! When Benny slipped into the deep burrow, he was surprised to find a small furry animal curled on the bottom. Startled at first when he saw it, he sniffed it and then punched it in the back with his front paw. The furry thing jumped in the air and slammed into the top of the burrow!

"Ouch," he yelled as he fell back to the floor. "Who are you and what are you doing in here. Can't you see I'm trying to sleep!"

"Well, that's a great way to greet me, since I'm the one who was born in this burrow and lived here with my mom and dad," Benny exclaimed.

"Sorry", the furry animal said rather sheepishly. "I didn't know who dug this, but I was glad to find it. I was out looking for my mother and father, but it was getting late. Then I saw this nice burrow and decided to sleep here for the night."

That's okay," Benny said, "it's big enough for the two of us. What are you, by the way?"

"I'm a coyote," he said rather proudly, as he puffed himself up to look bigger.

"A coyote?" Benny exclaimed, "Do you howl in the night like some of the other ones I have heard?"

"No, I don't do that!" he said, "Am I supposed to howl?"

"Well, most coyotes do howl, but if you feel like you need to do that, don't do it if I'm around," Benny answered. "It is very annoying in the middle of the night when I'm hunting because it scares all the little animals!"

"Say," he asked, "do you have a name? Mine's Benny!" the badger said as he stretched out to show he was bigger than the young coyote.

"Gee, I don't think I have one!" he answered. "Do I need one?"

"Sure, everyone needs a name. What if I wanted to call you? What would I say?"

"I don't know Benny. Why don't you give me a name?"

Benny thought for a minute and said, "I'll call you Furball, since that's what you are right now. A big ball of fur."

"Okay, I guess that would be nice to have a name! Thanks for doing that, Benny?"

"No problem, everyone needs a name, because, if I have to call you, I just can't say coyote or goofy or some odd name! You have to have one that we both know to be your own name."

Benny thought about it and looked again at Furball and decided it was okay to have another animal in his burrow. There was no one to talk to since his mother and father had left him alone, even if it was a coyote.

"Furball, would you like to stay here with me in the burrow?"

"Gee, that would be great, Benny. I don't have any friends, and my parents left me alone and didn't take me with them. So yes, that would be very nice of you, and we can become friends!"

"Look, it's getting late, and I want to sleep after coming all this way to be in my home burrow," Benny explained." It's been a long three days, and I'm excited to be able to sleep here for a change.

That night, they slept and had to sleep close to each other because the burrow was not very big for both of them. The young pup had always been with one of his family, especially when it was cold. So, at one point during the night, he slid over and fell asleep next to Benny to keep warm and cozy. When they awoke, they were surprised to be cuddled together, even though they were different animals in every way. It felt good to have the companionship.

Furball said, very sheepishly," Sorry, Benny, I was cold, and it was nice to sleep next to you and keep warm. Do you know that you snore and kick in your sleep!"

"No, I didn't know, Furball!" Benny said, "But that's what you get for sleeping next to me! I can fix that with a little more digging and increase the size of the burrow.

So, the two animals looked around and decided it needed to be bigger. They knew that both would grow in the months ahead, and they would need more room. Benny is a great digger, and he proceeded to scratch through the sandy, loam soil and worked efficiently to enlarge the burrow. Soon, he had a tunnel that ran under the old tree that had fallen down years ago. Then he made a big space at the end of the tunnel that would be his bedroom so Furball could have his own place to sleep. Furball was not good at digging, but he was good at moving the soil out of the hole and making a nice front entrance to their new home.

Both animals were happy about their work and rested during the day, and talked about how they were going to survive on their own. It was sad to be left alone at this young age, but they had found companionship with each other, even though they were quite different animals. They did have one thing in common: both liked to hunt at night, and with signals and techniques, they could be a great team. But for now, they needed something to eat!

"Benny," Furball asked, "How are we going to eat and get water? I'm hungry after all that work, so we need to do something before I faint!"

"Water is not a problem because there is a spring about 5 minutes away through the forest. I might have an idea about getting something to eat, though you may not like it, Furball!"

"Really, what's that, Benny? I could eat anything at this point, although I prefer something meaty, you know!"

"Okay, Furball, I am going to introduce you to a garden and great-tasting vegetables in the garden by that farmhouse. It's just on the other side of the pasture. It's not meat, but at this point we can't be choosy, right?"

The Garden

"I don't know Benny! I've never had vegetables before and never even heard of them. Already it doesn't sound very good!" Furball said with a quizzical look on his face.

Benny took Furball on top of the log, and they looked across the pasture where they could see a small white farmhouse with a large red barn where they kept a horse and two young calves. He knew about this because he would go there at night sometimes and catch mice that crawled around in the hay looking for some grain. It had been scattered by a young girl when she fed the animals in the morning on her way to school. Sometimes, if he was tired, he would sleep in the barn and creep out after she left, then he would sneak away and go to his burrow to sleep during the rest of the day.

She seemed like a nice girl, and he liked her because she was very gentle with the animals and brushed them every morning and sometimes in the afternoon. Usually, she would lead them around a fenced-in area to give them a little exercise and would talk to them all the time. The animals really liked her, and one of the calves would rest its head against the girl's arm so she would scratch it on the back. The calf would wiggle its body and swish its tail while the girl scratched its hind. It was fun to watch and made Benny sad that he didn't have someone like that in his life. This was the same girl that Benny had seen as she picked berries by the side of the road.

"I see it, Benny," Furball finally shouted! "I see a lot of green plants, but what are vegetables and what do they taste like?"

"Well, Furball," Benny responded, "They are very different from meat and all of them have a different taste. But you get used to it if you are hungry! Right now, I could use something in my tummy!"

" I don't know Benny. It doesn't sound very good to me." He said reluctantly to his new friend, "But you just never know about good things to eat! I might like them, so at least I'll try them!"

"Great Furball, you may become a vegetable eater after all!"

Benny explained what they needed to do, so the two animals worked their way across the open pasture and arrived at the fence by the garden. It had been put there to keep the cows and horses out of the garden. They were not designed to keep a badger and a coyote out, however. They both looked for any danger and then slipped under the bottom rail of the fence and entered the leafy jungle of plants.

It was a new and exciting experience for the coyote because he had never heard of a garden, much less one. He didn't know what there was to eat, so he followed his friend as he waddled through the rows of plants and stopped at one section. It had long, leaf-like tops and an orange plant that grew under the ground. Benny turned to Furball and motioned for him to be quiet as he pulled on one of the tops of the plant, and it popped out of the ground!

"Furball, this long orange thing is a carrot, and it tastes good. Here, try a bite!"

The coyote picked it up with his paws and rolled it around, and sniffed it as he did so. He looked at his friend and said, "Now what?"!

"Take a bite, Furball!" Benny exclaimed. "You'll like it, and besides, there's nothing else to eat except these vegetables. It will fill your stomach at least for a while!"

The coyote took a small bite from the end of the carrot, made a disgusting face, and spit it out! "This tastes awful," he said. "You might like to eat this green stuff, but I really can't stand it! Isn't there something else around here that might taste better?"

Benny smiled and said, "Furball, these are not that bad, and we have not had anything to eat for a few days now. You must give it a chance to taste the sweetness and enjoy the crunch when you bite into it. Besides, after this, we are going to the pea-pod part of the garden to try those sweet things."

"Oh no!" Furball exclaimed, "Not more of this green stuff to eat, Benny? You know, I can smell something I would eat coming from that fenced area over there. I can see some feathered animals scratching the ground and pecking. I bet they would taste good, don't you think?"

Benny looked in that direction and thought the same thing, but it looked dangerous because it was fenced, and there was a large multi-colored bird that was bigger than the rest that looked very mean. He turned to Furball and said, "You know you are probably right, but we can't take chances because I have seen the people in this farmhouse shoot a gun or something at my parents when they tried to get close to the birds. I was just a baby and had sneaked along behind them to see where they were going. It really scared me, and my parents ran away, and I was left by myself in the pasture. The sound of the gun was terrifying! That's the last I saw of my parents."

Despite his better judgment, Furball edged to the end of the garden and smelled the chickens and wondered what they tasted like. He was about to cross under the fence to get a closer look when he heard the farmhouse door open and a voice that yelled, "Get out of my garden, you lousy varmints!"

Both Benny and Furball quickly spun around with horrified looks on their faces. They quickly fled the garden and scooted under the fence that led to the pasture. They ran as fast as possible to seek cover in the tall grass and were soon hidden from view of the farmhouse. They stopped to catch their breath and looked back at the open doorway. A man stood there in overalls and a red flannel shirt. He held something that Benny knew was a gun.

The farmer raised his shotgun to shoot at them, but his daughter, Mary, said, "No, Daddy, don't shoot. They must have been hungry and really didn't take much. Besides, I think they're cute!"

The farmer looked at his daughter and smiled at her concern for the wild animals and said, "I may have to trap them and give them to the animal control people who will relocate them." He then aimed over their heads and fired the shotgun twice and watched as they scampered across the pasture.

Mary smiled and was glad her dad didn't shoot them, and thought *maybe I will go across the pasture and have a picnic. I'll take my favorite doll, Monica, with me one day soon. I bet they live somewhere close to that old fallen tree in the oak grove.*

Lunch with Monica

About three days later, Mary asked her mother if she could go on a picnic with her doll. "Mom, could you pack a nice big sandwich for me because I'm very hungry. Her mother smiled and soon had Mary fully equipped for a picnic with a sandwich, fruit, and a couple of her favorite cookies.

"Now, where are you going, young lady?" her mother asked." I don't want you to be far away, and you must stay on the farm property where I can see you."

"Okay, Mama, I'll be just across the pasture under that large oak tree. It's safe there and has a nice area to lay out my big blanket and set Monica up against the tree. She can be my companion for lunch. Monica likes to sit under a tree, and so do I. We won't be long!"

"Okay, honey, I can see you from the upstairs window anyway, so have fun!"

Mary gathered her blanket in her backpack along with Monica and carried the small lunch basket across the pasture to her favorite spot. All the while, she thought she might see the dog-looking animal and the low, squatty one with the black and white stripes. *Wouldn't that be fun, she thought, to see the small animals where they lived?*

She sat at the oak tree that she had arrived at, and she carefully laid out the blanket and placed Monica against the tree like she always did. "Now, Monica," Mary said with a stern voice. "Don't make a lot of noise because you may scare the animals away, since I think they live around here close by." Then she made Monica shake her head up and down as if she was saying, "Yes, I understand, and I'll be quiet!"

Mary carefully opened her basket and took out the big sandwich her mother had prepared for her. Then she talked to Monica about the two funny-looking animals she had seen the other day running across the pasture. She was amused that they were totally different animals, but they seemed to be friends.

Furball, who was dozing by the front entrance to the burrow, slowly awoke to the scent of food, which smelled wonderful. It had to be close by, so he poked his head up and looked over the entrance of his burrow at the young girl, who was sitting about thirty feet away under a tree. There was another person sitting against the tree that never moved, which seemed odd to him. He ducked back inside just as the girl looked up and saw him.

"*Oh, my goodness,*" He thought, very quietly as he slid back into the burrow. "*What if that young person saw me and wants to kill me?*"

So Furball ran through the connecting tunnel and then tumbled into Benny's chamber. He landed with a thud on top of the badger. Benny, who was in the middle of a great dream, jumped sideways as the coyote started babbling about a young girl outside the burrow.

"What are you doing, Furball!" Benny said very loudly. "You really scared me, you fool!"

"Benny, you will not believe it, but that young girl from the farmhouse is sitting outside the burrow and eating something that smells very good! There's another person sitting there with her, but it is not moving and doesn't say anything. Do you think the other person is dead? It's strange, Benny!" The excited coyote exclaimed!

"You are saying the girl from the farmhouse is sitting outside the burrow right now? And there is someone else with her? Are you sure she saw you, Furball? That could be scary if she did, because then we would not be safe here. She may tell her father where we are!"

"I know she saw me because she smiled at me and seemed to wave something in her hand that looked like food to me!"

"Furball, everything you look at seems like food to you! Maybe I should have a look myself just to make sure."

Benny slowly moved towards the entrance of the burrow and quickly peeked over the mound of dirt. Sure enough, there was the girl he had seen at the farmhouse eating a sandwich and talking to a small person sitting against the tree. As he lay there looking, she suddenly looked up and saw Benny. He quickly retreated into the burrow and thought about going out the other end of the tunnel. Then he heard a giggle and a voice that began to sing the same song he had heard when she was picking berries. He stopped and slid back to the entrance and noticed the girl had moved closer and had thrown a part of her sandwich in front of the burrow. Benny was now very afraid that it might be a trap, so he retreated further into the tunnel.

"Furball," Benny exclaimed. "I think she just threw some food in front of the entrance! I'm afraid it might be a trap, so we need to be very careful about reaching for it!"

"Food! I'm so hungry I don't care, Benny!" Furball exclaimed, and he raced up the tunnel and grabbed part of the sandwich by the entrance. Then he turned quickly and ran back where Benny was hidden. "Look, Benny, food, and it tastes great. Here, take some for yourself!"

Both the animals smiled and quickly ate the piece of sandwich the young girl had thrown at them. Soon they heard a voice from across the pasture calling the girl's name. The young girl answered and packed up her basket and turned to leave. As she did so she looked back and smiled at the two animals who stared at her from the entrance to the burrow. They seemed to be waiting for some more food. She reached into her basket and tossed the remaining part of her sandwich to them.

One night, Furball and Benny were looking for food and discovered that the coyote had an increased sense of smell and could detect the presence of small animals. If they were hiding, underground, or at the base of trees in the forest, Benny would dig furiously under the tree or into the burrow and chase the animal out the other side where furball would catch them.

On the way back to their own burrow, Furball looked at Benny and said "Benny this is a great way to hunt. I can smell the prey and you can dig the hole and scare them out!"

Benny looked at furball with a smile on his face and said, "yes furball that's a great idea and will do it again in a couple nights after we get some sleep today."

The two friends continued and happily climbed into their burrow to sleep during the day, and to go out again at night to hunt for food. This became the routine for the two friends to roam the woods looking for prey.

One morning Furball got up early to scout through the woods and looked for possible places where they could hunt. Then he and Benny could find some prey for the next night. He let his friend sleep because he was the one doing all the digging while they were hunting. Furball knew he was tired from the work he did the night before.

The Coyotes

He sensed there were other animals in the area. He could smell they were coyotes! Furball hid behind a bush but in an instant a large male coyote confronted him and bared its teeth with a throaty growl. Furball instinctively growled back but continued to back up towards his burrow that was 100's of yards away.

Then he noticed other coyotes that emerged from the underbrush. There were about 10 of them with older females and some young males and females. Their leader approached Furball slowly as he seemed to gauge whether the other coyote would just run away. He prepared to charge Furball who, while fully grown, had never been in a fight and this dominant male was very frightful.

About that time, Benny, who was enjoying a nice dream in his burrow, began hearing growling and snapping teeth somewhere outside their home. He first looked around for Furball and noticed the coyote was gone. He crept to the entrance of the burrow and looked around to see what had happened to his friend. Benny could hear Furball and another strange male coyote growling and snapping their teeth. Benny ran in the direction of the noise and saw a dominant male as he prepared to charge his friend.

Benny saw that his friend was in trouble and, without a second thought, charged across the forest floor and ran headlong into the surprised coyote. It turned and ran when it saw Benny's sharp claws and bared teeth and heard this scary sound of the badger as it ran directly at him.

Suddenly, there was a gunshot, and two men emerged from the woods and fired their guns at the fleeing coyotes. Both Benny and Furball quickly ducked back under some brush and lay still as the other coyotes scattered through the woods.

"That was scary with the large coyote and then the men with guns that shot at them!" Furball exclaimed as he shook with fear. I hope the men didn't see us hiding and don't come after us also!"

"I know, Furball, that was a close call, first with the large coyote and then the men and their guns. It's been a very scary day for sure! I think we should hide out here until we think it might be safe and then go back outside to see if anyone was hurt."

After an hour, they knew the men had left, so the two friends sneaked out the back exit of the burrow and carefully looked around.

Benny saw something moving and went there to investigate. It was a small coyote, and it seemed to be unconscious. "Furball, I think this young coyote hit his head on this branch and knocked himself out. I think we should drag it back into our and burrow to keep it safe in case the men do come back!'

The friends dragged the unconscious coyote to the safety of the burrow. It was then that they realized that the coyote was a young female. Furball poked the coyote to see if he could wake her up. She slowly opened her eyes and let out a loud yip, and then tried to run away, but Benny blocked the exit. She realized there was no escape, so she bit Furball.

"Ouch," He yelled, "That hurts! We saved you, and that's what you do; Bite me! She then started to cry, but he grabbed her, and she lay still in one of the sleeping areas.

Furball and Benny tried to talk to her and calm the young coyote down. It was obvious she was terrified being in a strange place and looking at the ferocious black and white striped creature with long claws and sharp teeth. Furball understood her fear and gently moved her to an area that was away from Benny. When the two coyotes were in a separate part of the burrow, Furball asked her gently, "What's your name?"

Nervously, the young coyote said, "Camille, at least that's what they call me. What's your name?"

"My friend here is called Benny, and he calls me Furball because that's what I looked like when I was just born. I know that sounds funny, but that has been my name as long as I have lived. I really like it because it was given to me by my best friend, the badger."

"I've never seen a badger before, and he looks very mean and dangerous!" she said very nervously.

"No, Camille; He's my friend because we grew up together in this burrow. We even hunt together and are good at finding food to eat. Maybe you can come along and watch us one night soon. For now, you should rest because you really hurt your head when you hit that branch. It must have been scary when the men started to shoot at you."

Camille seemed to be calmer and, in a very sweet way, reached out her paw to touch Furball on the cheek and say, "It's nice to know you, Furball." She looked down the tunnel and saw the badger as he sat and watched the two coyotes. "It's also nice to meet you as well, Benny!"

Benny sat back and watched the two coyotes talk to each other and smiled that his friend had found another coyote. Perhaps she might become his mate one day. But as he smiled, Benny thought to himself, it would be nice if there were another badger that would be his mate. They could hunt together and maybe even have a family of their own.

All three animals were exhausted by the day's activities and curled up in a ball and went to sleep. At one point in the middle of the night, Benny awoke and looked at the two coyotes who were cuddled together as if they were one.

After a few days of hunting together, Benny knew that Camille and Furball were going to be together forever. He knew they might soon decide to leave him and go away to start a life on their own. This made him sad, but also happy for his friend.

For the next month, the three animals hunted together as a team and were very successful in feeding themselves. It became more evident that both Camille and Furball would be a couple for life.

So, one day, Furball came to Benny and said, "Benny, Camille, and I have been thinking about raising a family of our own. We need to find the other coyotes and be a part of their pack as well. "

Benny was sad and looked at the two coyotes and said, "I wish you all the best in your life, but please come back and visit me one day. I will be in this burrow for as long as I live. "

Both Camille and Furball walked up to Benny and gave him a big hug, especially Furball. He put his arms around Benny's neck and gave him a hard squeeze and told him he would miss him very much. Then, both coyotes scampered off into the night and disappeared through the Grove of oak trees in search of Camille's family.

A Mate for Benny

Now Benny was alone again, and without the company of Furball. He was fully grown and was a ferocious animal to deal with in the forest. Most of the other predators in the woods knew this and stayed away from the badger when he was hunting.

One day, as Benny searched for food, he smelled a different scent in the air. It seemed to be coming from a fallen oak tree on the other side of a small clearing. He silently approached the tree and climbed to the top of the log, ready to pounce on whatever was on the other side. But as he prepared to jump, he realized it was another badger. It was a small animal and seemed to be having a problem breathing. Benny slid off the log and approached the badger, which was lying on its side. He realized immediately that the smaller badger was a female and looked as if it had not eaten in several days.

Benny scurried back to his burrow, where he had some food stored, and quickly brought it back to the female badger. She seemed to smell the food and began to eat it slowly. At first, she just lay there after eating food, but then she slowly rolled over onto her feet. She looked up at the large badger and, with a weak smile, said, "Thank you very much for the food. I didn't know there were any other badgers that lived around here. I lost my way and have been travelling for several days, far away from my home. I thought I was going to die lying here."

She then turned in and said, "Thanks again for the help. I do appreciate the food, but I must find my parents. They have gone off somewhere, and I don't know where to look!"

"That's what happened to me when my parents left when I was just a young badger! I had to find my way for food and shelter and have survived for a couple of seasons on my own."

He was pleased to have found another badger that he could talk to, and maybe be a part of his family. He motioned for her to follow him to a small pond, which had recently formed from the recent rainfall. She drank for a while, and then with her paws, washed her face and body in the cool water.

Looking back at Benny, she said, "My name is Beatrice, but my parents always call me Bea before they left me! What's your name?"

"I'm Benny, and it's very nice to meet you. I wonder if you would like to stay in my burrow. Then, when you are stronger, we can decide what you want to do about your parents. There's plenty of room, because when I was younger, I met a coyote, and he and I shared this burrow. As he and I grew, we needed to make the area bigger. So we became good friends and lived together for a long time. "

"You became friends with a coyote?" She exclaimed, "They can be dangerous if they hunt together in a pack! I have heard them howling at the full moon, and it scares me to hear that sound."

"Well, he's not here any longer since he found a mate several months ago when a pack of coyotes tried to attack us. Then some men tried to shoot them and scared them off, but one of the small females was left behind after she hit a branch and was unconscious. So, we dragged her into our burrow that night, where she slept until the morning. My friend's name is Furball, and the young female coyote's name is Camille. They became very close and soon left me to find her friends. "

Bea smiled and said, "Yes, I'd like very much to go to your burrow because I've slept beside this log for two days now. I want to be safe and secure, and next to another badger!"

The two badgers walked slowly in the direction of the burrow. But Bea was still weak and had to take it slowly. They soon arrived at the entrance, and Bea smiled as she looked at the extensive work Benny had done to provide a comfortable and secure home. She smiled and looked at Benny happily.

She immediately slid down the hall and found a very comfortable spot among the dry leaves and said, "Benny, thank you very much for saving my life and for sharing your home with me tonight." She then drifted off to sleep.

Benny sat across from her and watched her sleep. Perhaps this might be the mate that he's been waiting for all this time. Benny fell asleep, but found himself being awakened in the early afternoon by Bea because she was getting hungry again.

Benny smiled and said, "You will have to wait till evening, and then we'll sneak across the pasture to a garden by the farmhouse on the other side of the pasture. I hope you like carrots, he said, with a smile!"

The sun had gone down for a couple of hours, and darkness completely enveloped the woods and the pasture beyond as they approached the garden. Benny said quietly, "You must be careful here because the man in the house has a gun and he will shoot at us if he finds us in the garden. So, we must take a few vegetables and carry them back under the fence and back to our burrow to eat. "

Bea nodded that she understood, and the two of them slid under the barbed wire fence and made their way to the carrots. Benny realized it had been a while since he had been back to the garden, and the carrots were fully grown now. He motioned to Bea to just take one, and he would take another. Then they would leave the garden quietly. They slipped under the fence rather awkwardly and dragged the large carrots behind them.

 Little did they know that the young girl in the farmhouse saw them sneaking away, and smiled broadly, knowing that her badger had found a friend. In two days, it would be the weekend and she would pack another picnic lunch and go back to her spot under the oak tree. She could hardly wait to see the two of them together and tease them out of their burrow for a bite of sandwich or a piece of fruit.

Another picnic and a Rescue

Saturday came and the sun was shining brightly in the blue sky with small, puffy clouds that seemed to be suspended in space. Mary approached her mother and said she wanted to have another picnic in the woods like before.

As before, her mother packed an orange, and a nice sandwich for her picnic lunch, but Mary insisted that her mother put a small sandwich in the basket for her doll Monica. Her mother smiled at Mary and followed her wishes for her favorite doll. She then told her to be careful, but knew that her daughter was very resourceful, and would not get into trouble. Her mother also knew she could watch her daughter to make sure she was safe.

Mary arrived at the tree and set her doll up against the tree and then laid out her picnic lunch. It wasn't long before Benny could smell the food that was laid out on the blanket. He remembered the first time that Furball met the girl and she fed them. He wondered if the same would be true for him.

Slowly, he stuck his head out of the burrow, and at first, the young girl was afraid because the badger was quite large now. Benny bowed his head respectfully, and she seemed to understand that the badger would not hurt her. She took a piece of her sandwich and threw it in the general direction of Benny. He looked at the food, and then at the girl, and back at the food again. He slowly crept out of the burrow, grabbed it with his long paws, and scurried back into the depths of the burrow.

He smiled at Bea and gave her a piece of meat wrapped in bread. She smelled it and smiled and then ate it quickly. It was the first time she had eaten food that was made by a human. It was very tasty and filled her stomach.

"That was really good, Benny!" She exclaimed. "Does she come here often?"

"Not regularly, but when she does, she always leaves us some food to eat."

When they had finished, Benny went up to the entrance of the burrow and saw that the young girl had packed up her lunch basket and started back across the pasture. But as he looked back at the tree where she had been sitting, there was an orange and a small sandwich left behind. He smiled and quickly ran to the tree and gathered the leftover food for himself and Bea.

Benny was pleased that the girl would come to the tree again after Furball left and that he could share the food with Bea. He hoped that Bea would one day become his mate for life. After they had stored the food for later, Benny climbed on top of the old oak log and peered across the pasture as the girl skipped home through the tall grass. He smiled and thought she was a wonderful human that he could trust.

As he watched, however, he noticed the pasture grass moving as if an animal was following her. Benny ran higher up the log and could see the top of a coyote tail as it moved stealthily through the tall grass. He realized the coyote was stalking Mary. He ran down the log and headed across the pasture as fast as he could to attack the coyote and save Mary.

Mary was not aware of the danger that was behind her, but Benny knew he had to stop the coyote from harming the young girl. As he approached the girl, he could see the coyote on the pathway getting ready to pounce on her. He charged through the tall pasture grass and emitted a fearsome growl that scared the girl and alerted the coyote that there was trouble behind him.

The badger has very sharp teeth, but so does the coyote. The difference is that the badger's skin is very thick, and the hair matted down was a defensive system from most animals' attacks. Benny lunged at the coyote, knocked it to the ground, bit deeply into its leg, and cut its sides with his sharp claws. The Coyote tried to bite the badger, but it could not break through the skin. The coyote realized it was beaten and rolled over in the grass, and broke free from Benny's grasp. It ran quickly back to the woods as Benny watched it leave.

The young girl screamed and ran towards the house as fast as she could and yelled for her mother. Benny could see the older woman in the house as she ran out the door towards her daughter. She picked Mary up and ran to the safety of the house. Benny noticed that Mary had dropped her doll when she ran, and it lay in the grass in front of him. He gently picked it up in its jaws and walked slowly towards the house. He was fearful that he might be shot for coming close to the home, but he had to bring the doll back to the girl.

At first, Mary thought the badger was going to eat her doll, but her mother calmed her and told her to watch and wait.

"Let's wait and see what the badger does, honey. He doesn't look like he is going to hurt Monica." Her mother said as they watched from the window.

With tears in her eyes for her beloved doll, she watched as the badger placed the doll against the fence post in a seated position. It was just like the girl had done at the tree in the woods. Benny then turned and ran back through the grass to his home. He had an interesting story to tell Bea, who was waiting in the burrow for him.

A Badger Family

Six months had passed, and Bea gave birth to their son, whom they named Anthony. He was a cute little badger in the beginning, but after a few weeks, he was crawling all over the burrow and tearing into things and digging his own tunnel just for fun. Both Benny and Bea enjoyed watching the young badger learning some of the skills necessary for his later life. Feeding him was a chore, however, since Benny had to do all the hunting and bring home food for Bea and Tony. One day, he noticed honeybees flying past when he was far away from his normal hunting area. He tried to follow them but couldn't find the beehive. He vowed that he would come back another day to look for it.

A few days later, Benny returned to the area where he had seen the bees and followed them as they approached a hollowed-out log on the forest floor. Surely that had to be the spot for the beehive. He began scratching around the base of the old log, and soon there were 100s of bees buzzing around the badger, trying to sting him. They needed to keep him away from the hive. But badgers have such thick skin and coarse hair covering it that the bees are not able to sting any part of the badger. Benny opened the log with his powerful front paws and could see the interior of the hive with the honeycombs and, more importantly, the larvae, or bee eggs, which were his favorite. He ate the larvae, and when he was full, he decided to break off part of a honeycomb and bring it back to Bea and Tony.

When he arrived at the front of the burrow, he called out to Bea and Tony to come out to see the surprise he brought them. "This is honey I found in a log", he said with a proud smile. "You will like this very much!"

Bea was thrilled to have the honey, and Tony was excited to have such a sweet treat as he licked the honey off the waxy honeycomb. After he finished, he chewed the waxy material and made a mess in the burrow. It was so bad that Benny had to redo the entrance to remove the wax and sticky honey that was on the ground.

Smiling, both Bea and Benny lay down while watching Tony dig another tunnel just for fun. Soon, though, Tony became weary and settled down next to his mother and fell fast asleep. And so, it went for the badger family; hunting at night and sleeping most of the day. Occasionally, Benny would wonder what had happened to his old friend Furball. It had been a long time since they were together, and he missed his old friend.

In another part of the forest, a couple of miles away, Furball and Camille had joined other coyotes with friends and family. He wondered also what had happened to Benny and thought about someday traveling back to the old burrow to see if he was still there. But for now, though, the pups were young and couldn't travel, so they stayed with the group and hunted for food together.

Many months passed, and his family had grown, and the pack of coyotes was larger, which made hunting for food more difficult. Furball remembered how he and Benny worked as a team to catch prey, with the badger digging and the coyote waiting for the animal to come out. They were great together, and he really missed his old friend. One day, there was a fight over food that he had caught for his family. It was ripped away from him by two larger male coyotes. That night, he talked to Camille, and they decided to go out on their own and maybe even see if they could find Benny.

As the rest of the pack slept, Furball, Camille, and their three pups slipped away and headed towards the area where Benny and the coyote had first lived. They had to stay hidden during the day because farmers didn't like coyotes and might shoot them.

It was a long way to the old area where both Benny and Furball had grown up. The pups, however, complained about the distance, but at least kept the pace. It had grown very dark now, and the forest seemed to close in on them as they walked along the path. Soon, they came to a stream that Furball remembered was close to the old Burrow. He was pleased that he had been able to at least find this part of the forest and knew that they were close to their old burrow.

Soon they arrived at the burrow only to find it was empty. "I don't know where my friend the badger is, but at least we can sleep here for the night and look around again tomorrow. "

Everyone was tired from the long trek through the dark and scary forest, so they used his old home to spend the night, where they could get much-needed rest. Furball went to the entrance of the burrow and wondered where Benny might have gone.

The next evening, there was a full moon, and Furball drifted outside the burrow and howled at the bright, yellow orb in the sky just as he had done with the other coyotes. He  recalled Benny telling him that if he wanted to howl at night, to go somewhere else and do it! It would disturb the other small animals that they were hunting. He laughed to himself, thinking of Benny, when suddenly there was a crashing sound coming through the brush next to the log, and there was Benny in all his glory!

At first, the two animals stared at each other, and then, in a rush, hugged each other and rejoiced that they had found themselves together again.

The Reunion

"You're all grown up, Furball!" Benny exclaimed.

"Yes, of course, and better yet, remember that coyote we found a long time ago by the name of Camille? Well, she's now my mate for life, and we have three pups that are six months old. They hunt with us now, but I still have to do all the work!" He said with a proud smile.

"Furball; that's great, and I have a mate as well. Her name is Bea, and I have a young badger named Anthony. He's not quite ready for the nightly hunting, but should be ready soon. I take him with me to show him how to do things, and he's a fast learner." Benny proudly said as he looked towards the bushes where his family had hidden. He motioned for Bea and Anthony to come out to meet Furball.

"This is my family, and I want to meet yours, too, Furball. Are they close by?"

"I left them in our old burrow when I came out to see the moon and howl a little bit. I'll run back and get them!"

Furball scurried off, and within a few minutes, Benny and his family were surrounded by coyotes, big and small. Anthony had never seen a coyote and hid behind his mother. But one of the young pups trotted over to sniff the young badger. Anthony reared back and showed his young, but sharp teeth and claws hidden under the fur of his front paws. The young coyote jumped back and ran into one of his sisters, who had followed him over to see what he was doing.

"Come here and meet each other," Benny said to everyone. "Your father and I lived together for a long time and hunted almost every night for food as a team. Maybe you all can become a team when you're a little older?"

After a few minutes of getting acquainted, they began playing and rolling in the dirt and into the bushes, giggling and laughing. Furball and Benny and their mates sat and watched their young offspring and smiled at each other.

Benny finally said. "Furball, why don't you stay close by, and we can hunt together again and teach our youngsters to do the same. Our old burrow seems to fit your family, and if not, I will help you make it even bigger."

Benny, that's a great idea, but let me talk to Camille about it. You know we have left our pack forever, and I can't think of anyone I would rather be around than you!"

And so it went; the badgers and coyotes lived close to each other; totally different animals, but with a common purpose to raise their families in peace and harmony. They were loving neighbors and living with nature in the area they called Bearberry Pass!

BENNY THE BADGER

Honey Badger

Badgers have long cavities in their skulls, which gives resistance to jaw dislocation and increases their bite grip strength. This, in turn, limits jaw movement to hinging open and shut, or sliding from side to side, but it does not hamper the twisting movement that rips into the prey.

Badgers have rather short, wide bodies, with short legs for digging. They have elongated, weasel-like heads with small ears. Their tails vary in length depending on species and age. They have black faces with distinctive white markings, grey bodies with a light-colored stripe from head to tail, and dark legs with light-colored underbellies. They grow to around 90 cm (35 in) in length, including the tail.

The European badger is one of the largest; the American badger, the hog badger, and the honey badger are generally a little smaller and lighter. They weigh around 9–11 kg (20–24 lb.), while some Eurasian badgers weigh around 18 kg (40 lb.).

The behavior of badgers differs by family, but all shelter underground, living in burrows called setts, which may be very extensive. They are fast diggers and can dig tunnels even in the hardest ground. They range in depths up to 10 feet. Some are solitary, moving from home to home, while others are known to form clans called cetes. Cete size is variable from two to 15. The gestation period of a female badger is about six 6 months, and they usually have only one or two cubs.

Badgers can run or gallop at 25–30 km/h (16–19 mph) for short periods of time. They are nocturnal in nature.

In North America, coyotes sometimes eat badgers and vice versa, but most of their interactions seem to be mutual or neutral. American badgers and coyotes have been seen hunting together in a cooperative fashion.

American badgers catch a significant proportion of their food underground by digging. They can tunnel after ground-dwelling rodents at speed. They are mainly carnivorous and will attack any other animal with fury that overwhelms the prey, which even includes poisonous snakes that have little if any effect on the badger when bitten.

Their main enemies are a pack of coyotes, a mountain lion, or mankind. In Africa, they can become prey to the African leopard or larger snakes, as well as lions and hyenas.

Coyote

The **coyote** is a species of canine native to North America. It is smaller than its close relative, the wolf, and slightly smaller than the closely related eastern wolf and red wolf. The coyote is larger and more predatory and was once referred to as the **American jackal** by a behavioral ecologist.

The coyote is listed as of least concern by the International Union for Conservation of Nature, due to its wide distribution and abundance throughout North America. The species is versatile, able to adapt to and expand into environments modified by humans; urban coyotes are common in many cities.

The coyote has 19 recognized subspecies. The average male weighs 8 to 20 kg (18 to 44 lb.) and the average female 7 to 18 kg (15 to 40 lb.). Their fur color is predominantly light gray and red, interspersed with black and white, though it varies somewhat with geography. It is highly flexible in social organization, living either in a family unit or in loosely knit packs of unrelated individuals.

Primarily carnivorous, its diet consists mainly of deer, rabbits, rodents, and birds, even fish. However, it may also eat fruits and vegetables on occasion. Its characteristic vocalization is a howl made by solitary individuals. Humans are the coyote's greatest threat, followed by cougars and gray wolves. Despite predation by gray wolves, coyotes sometimes mate with them, and with eastern, or red wolves, producing "coywolf" hybrids.

The coyote is a prominent character in Native American folklore, usually depicted as a trickster that alternately assumes the form of an actual coyote or a man. As with other trickster figures, the coyote uses deception and humor to rebel against social conventions. The animal was especially respected in some cultures as a symbol of military might. Wolves, however, are seen as their public image improves, while attitudes towards the coyote remain largely negative.

The coyote is strictly monogamous, even in areas with high coyote densities and abundant food. During the pregnancy, the male frequently hunts alone and brings back food for the female. The female may line the den with dried grass or with fur pulled from her belly. The gestation period is 63 days, with an average litter size of six, which relates to the density of the pack and the abundance of food.

Acknowledgement

It is difficult for me to write about animals in the wild without leaning heavily on my own experiences as a child, but the great research one can find in Wikipedia. It is a robust source of material on many subjects, especially in the natural world. I also acknowledge the introduction to the area outside Bearberry Pass north of San Antonio,

Texas. This is truly a work of fiction and was a fun book to write and eventually publish.

About The Author

Michael Rubel graduated from The United States Naval Academy in 1963, from which there is no better institution that teaches a young man honor, ethics, integrity and a moral commitment to himself and the country. Today The U. S, Naval Academy graduate's men and women that put their country and others first in all they do in life. Many of the graduates continue through the officer ranks and are captains and admirals and endure the separation from home as they pursue the naval career. Others resign, after the required time, to serve, and become sought after by industry for their intelligence but more, their integrity, commitment to purpose and work ethic.

The author now lives in Southern California, with his wife of many years, while pursuing his writing ambitions that entail children's books, a short, animated film, a script for a western movie as well as his YouTube series, "Letters from the Edge" by author Mike Rubel, a compilation about life, of what we would call humanity. He can be reached at: booksbyrubel@gmail.com

Made in the USA
Coppell, TX
14 January 2026

69160888R00031